Lara's
First Christmas

What a strange sight we must have made—the sturdy old grandfather of
a man in his leather apron and the little girl in the boy's knickers....

Lara's First Christmas

Alice O. Howell

Illustrations by Maggie Mailer

BELL POND BOOKS
2004

Story copyright Alice O. Howell 2004
Illustrations copyright Maggie Mailer 2004

Published by Bell Pond Books
400 Main Street
Great Barrington, MA

www.steinerbooks.org

Library of Congress Cataloging in Publication data is available.

10 9 8 7 6 5 4 3 2 1

Printed in the United States of America

With loving memory of

my darling husband

"Polar Bear,"

a.k.a. Walter Alfred Andersen

M ANY YEARS AGO, in fact before World War II, I discovered Christmas. It happened the winter my parents decided to go to Norway. I was nine years old. We first spent a week in a hotel in Oslo. To this very day I do not know why they suddenly decided to go on to Finse. Certainly it was not to ski, since neither of them knew how to ski, nor could it have been just for pleasure. Perhaps it was necessary for political reasons that my father drop out of sight for a while. All I remember is that one morning we got up in the dark, packed our few belongings in our battered suitcases, and had to be down for breakfast in a hurry, because we had to catch the early train to Bergen.

It was cold, and I was most unhappy at being ripped from a nice warm bed.

When we went down to the hotel dining room we found it unlit and deserted—a sea of empty tables with white tablecloths, dully gleaming flatware, and baskets of rolls. A sleepy waiter appeared and turned on a section of lights. He seemed quite disgruntled at being summoned so early, and drew back the long, heavy curtains crossly with a swish and clink of their brass rings. Outside it was still night. You could see the streetlight shining through

the ever-falling snow. I remember I had some toast with orange marmalade, and my mouth tasted very odd after eating it. And it was still dark when we left in a taxi for the station. Both my parents seemed silent and tense. I dared not ask them where we were going.

I was getting used to these sudden departures—always westward—to strange places. Sometimes we were in big grey cities in Europe and recently we had been surrounded by desert, camels, and  palm trees as we went from villages to towns across Egypt and North Africa. We never stayed anywhere longer than three months, and I grew accustomed to strange, unintelligible languages and even stranger kinds of food. I spent hours just watching people as I sat on suitcases waiting for my father to buy tickets and exchange one kind of money for another. I would try to read the billboards in different alphabets and explain them secretly to Alfred, a ratty and much-loved stuffed bear who was my best friend and only toy, since everything we owned had to fit into three suitcases. Sometimes I would try and try to remember where home had originally been. It was somewhere far to the East. We never spoke of it. I could only barely picture a long grey wooden fence, green grass and birch trees, and a laundry line full of flapping sheets and towels. And the sense of safety. Safety is always a pretty green and white when I think about it.

I also remember a gypsy with a dancing bear who came to our village.

Anyway, we did catch the train in time, and when the sun rose—which was late in the morning in those latitudes—we were winding up through mountains covered with spruce trees. Here the snow had stopped, the clear air was glistening, and as the train curved back on itself, the white smoke from the locomotive made a beautiful pattern against the bright blue sky.

The train climbed higher and higher, moving more slowly with the strain. I listened to the sounds of the wheels on the track. They seemed to be saying, "potato-packer, potato-packer, potato-packer," sometimes slowly, then sometimes faster. I thought it was funny and started to chant it to myself, rocking to and fro, but my mother held up a warning finger—I was never to draw attention to us—so I stopped and looked out the window again. I noticed that the trees seemed to be getting shorter and shorter. Finally, they disappeared altogether as we rose above the tree line and emerged on the top of a rolling desert of brilliant snow dunes. All was blindingly white. I had to squint. My mother must have anticipated this, because she fished in her large purse and took out a pair of sun goggles. "Here, Lara," she cautioned me, "put these on and remember to wear them whenever you set foot out the door or you could become snow-blind. Promise me faithfully—and for heaven's sake, don't lose them!" In answer to my look of concern, she added that she and my father would be wearing them, too.

I put the goggles on—they were attached to a broad band of black elastic—and I looked out the window again. Now everything was washed with a golden tint and looked even more beautiful.

My parents then put on their own goggles, which

made them look like insects. I had to giggle in spite of myself. It certainly rendered them "incognito," a word I had come to learn from overhearing them talk. It meant that people would not recognize them and know who they were.

My mother also explained that because of the dazzling light and dry cold, I was no longer required to wash my face. Instead, I was to clean it only with cold cream. I could easily get sunburned. Just then the train stopped with a great shudder, shake, and a long squeal. A sign outside read "FINSE." We were in such haste to get off, I almost forgot Alfred, but the conductor laughed and said that we had plenty of time.

We were the only people to get off the train. Some sacks of provisions were thrown out of the baggage car and men shouted agreeably to each other. The train stood like an enormous beast beside us, sweating and steaming and emitting deep rumblings. The engineer waved a large gloved hand out the window at me, and I waved back politely, which was difficult with so many things to carry.

When the train groaned and pulled away, we were left standing in a wilderness. There was no village—no streets, no shops, no inhabitants. There was only an open shed with lumber in it and a large wooden station house which had been painted dark red. The snow piled up in places as high as the second-story windows and a

narrow pathway had been dug between steep walls of snow to the doorway. Over the entrance I could now see a sign reading "HOTEL FINSE." Apparently, we had arrived at our destination.

When we went inside, the place seemed quite cozy. A hall led straight to a back entrance. There was a lounge, which they called the "salon," with armchairs and tables, and a dining room with wooden chairs, which were carved and painted with colorful hearts and leaves. Grown-ups would describe the place as having a "rustic decor," which means it was peasanty on purpose. There was a big stove made of china in one corner of the salon and a small triangular bar in the other. Glass shelves stood behind it with bottles and little fancy dolls between the bottles. The pictures on the walls were paintings of blue mountains and steep green meadows dropping to narrow pointed bays called *fjords*. People could sit there and think about summertime while they looked out the windows at all the snow.

The proprietress, who wore a lovely embroidered apron, led us upstairs. She was very plump and had yellow braids around her head. Briskly, with many Norwegian words and sweeping gestures, she showed us to our rooms. To my dismay I found that my room was quite far from that of my parents. In fact, it was along several further bends in the narrow corridor. It was the first time that I was to be separated from them by such a distance. I begged to be allowed to sleep on a cot in their room. But this was not to be. The proprietress seemed to express shock that I would be such a little scaredy-cat.

My room had a narrow wooden bed with a down comforter puffed up on it. Opposite it, there was a stand holding a blue and white china bowl and pitcher for washing. A frayed little carpet peeped out from under a straight-backed chair and a chest of drawers. I could see a chamber pot under the bed.

After I had hidden Alfred under the comforter, I looked out the window and realized that I was at the back of the hotel and thus had a glorious view of the mountains off in the distance. They looked like mounds of whipped cream. There was not even a speck of rock showing. In front of them was a flat surface which suggested a frozen lake, and twisting down the nearest mountain in a clumpy way on the far side of the lake was something shining the palest of robin's-egg blue. It proved to be a glacier. I also noticed that the snow was conveniently piled high right outside my window, and I soon learned to save myself the trouble of running down the stairs by simply climbing out the window and sliding down on my bottom.

There seemed to be only a very few guests. The ones I remember best were two antique and aristocratic Englishmen. They had titles. One of them looked like a horse and the other looked like a badger. Both of them were skinny in different ways, but had the same wispy grey hair and droopy mustaches. Both wore tweed knickers, heavy woolen socks and huge boots, and were given to wearing identical checkered woolly

scarves and old Norfolk jackets over their thick hand-knitted jerseys when they went out to "shee," as they pronounced the word "ski." They had taken to this sport long before it was a sport. In those days, the Norwegians skied because they had to. It was the only way of getting from one place to the other. The Englishmen skied because they liked to—they were obviously ahead of their time. Later I discovered that in other parts of Norway, the women had straight-backed chairs mounted on long metal runners, which they could load up with a baby or packages and push up the road. When the road sloped down, they could straddle the flexible runners and coast down the hill. It still seems to me a most sensible arrangement and even fun for old ladies. I wish I had one today!

We settled in, and as the days passed, the kindly English gentlemen somehow produced a pair of small skis and ski poles for me. They took the greatest pleasure in patiently teaching me the rudiments of getting about. I was quite apt from the start, and I remember my pride and delight in skiing with them across that frozen lake and up the side of the extraordinary glacier. It was a frozen river of ice. They told me how very dangerous glaciers are and, holding me tightly by the back of my jacket, they showed me a deep crack in it, which they called a crevasse. As I looked down through the fierce blue-green ice to the cold black shadows in the depths, I shuddered. And I shuddered even more when they told me the story of the young man who had gone mountain climbing in Switzerland with a group of his friends. They were all members of the same club. The young fellow had fallen to his death down the deepest crevasse, and there was no way of retrieving the body. So when they got back to safety, they sat down and reckoned how long it would take the glacier to move to a spot where the body might be found again. It was something like forty years. They therefore agreed to meet again at that place

when the years would have elapsed. They kept their promise, but only a few of the friends were still living, and some were quite old by that time. The Englishmen described to me the poignancy of a handful of worn and wrinkled old men, such as themselves, actually coming across the body of the handsome youth for whom time had stopped and frozen.

I did not share any of this with my parents—for both seemed disinterested, sad, and withdrawn. I believe that my father would sometimes take the train to other places, always leaving and returning on the same day. He smoked many cigarettes and my mother knitted. They often sat without talking across from each other in the small, dark salon as if they were waiting for something that never came. Deliverance, perhaps.

✳   ✳   ✳   ✳

There is no doubt that I was left a good deal on my own, and since I was a naturally curious child, I took to exploring and poking about. It was not long before I discovered a door at the back of an alcove to the left of the entrance. This alcove was called the "Garderobe" and served as a place for the residents to hang their wet coats and jackets and take off their boots. The place reeked of damp wool, leather, and rubber and ski wax—nice masculine smells, I think even today. Actually, there were hardly any women in the hotel, except for the proprietress, my mother, and a chambermaid who doubled as a waitress at dinner. Perhaps there was a cook. I was certainly the only girl and the only child in the entire place. And though I kept active, I seemed to live in a constant aching void that I know now to be loneliness.

Now here, of a sudden, was a door. I pushed down the metal handle and opened it. Then I walked through into a mysterious space. It must have been a covered shed added on to the left of the hotel. From my viewpoint, though, it seemed to be a large unlit hall, an incredibly cold one, and with good reason. As my eyes became accustomed to the darkness, I could see that it contained a large enclosed skating rink, covered with a sheet of black ice. Nobody, apparently, was interested in skating. Across the ice was another open doorway. It formed a golden rectangle of light and looked inviting. Timidly, very timidly, I shuffled and slipped across the rink to the opening and peered in.

It was a carpenter's shop full of gleaming boards and odd bits of wood, which accounted for the golden light. There were also white curls of shavings and sawdust all over the floor. Seated in the midst of this, surrounded by all manner of tools of his trade, sat a carpenter—a large rosy-faced man with wire-rimmed spectacles and white tufts of hair over his ears. Otherwise he was bald. He wore a heavy leather apron over his clothes and was busy gluing two small bits of wood together with the greatest of care and precision. As I stood there on the threshold, he looked up and smiled. It was a great warm smile and lit up his face and filled it with craggy crinkles of kindness. I smiled back. His name, as it turned out, was Andreas. I had found a friend.

It is hard for me now to understand how it was so easy for us to converse. I spoke very little Norwegian, and he had not a word of French. He spoke, however, a bit of English, and he must have had a very good education. (French and English—rather than our native tongue which, for some reason, it was dangerous for us ever to speak—were the languages my parents and I had spoken for the last few years.) Nevertheless, Andreas and I certainly did communicate, because I have such fine memories of our conversations.

The first time, he invited me in by cupping his hands and waving them gently, drawing me towards him with a shy smile. He assumed, I think, that I was a boy, which at that age pleased me no end. No wonder he did so, since my brown hair was cropped short and fell over

my eyes like a pony's, and I lived day in
thick boys' knickers and choice of tw
overs. When he asked me my name anᵤ
"Lara," his eyes laughed with surprise, and he puₓ
his rough hand and pushed the hair back from my face
and apologized. I can still see how kind his expression
was and how appreciative he seemed of the fact that,
indeed, I was a little girl. The snow was flocking and
whirling outside the window behind him as he then
told me haltingly that years before he had lost his wife
and a daughter Kirsti, just my age, to a cruel epidemic
of influenza. This gave his tenderness towards me a very
special meaning.

I told no one of my discovery. I was learning to lead a
secret life of my own. Every day, as soon as I had finished
my breakfast, rolled up my nap-
kin and pushed it through its
wooden napkin ring, I would
excuse myself from the table
and make a beeline for my
room upstairs. Then I would
open my window, climb out
with the help of the chair, slide
down the snowchute my bottom
had worn in the snow, run through
the back door of the hotel, down the
hall and through the alcove and wet

coats, through the hidden door, across the ice in a skill-ful swoop, and into Andreas's arms. What good, pipe-smelling hugs he had for me! He would always press his hand to my forehead and smooth the hair back from it in that familiar gesture, telling me what a pretty "lilla Lara" I was, and what a lovely woman I was sure to grow up to be. Until then, I had never even given the matter a thought.

He asked me about my father and mother and did I have any brothers or sisters? And would I not like to make my mother a Christmas present because Christ-mas was coming soon? He called it "*Jul*" and pro-nounced this "yule." As ashamed as I felt, I confessed I did not know about Christmas. They never had it where I came from.

Andreas opened his eyes wide with shock and sur-prise. Then he paused to think a moment. With much care he explained that it was a most holy occasion and a time for gift-giving and rejoicing. It was a time, he said, when God gave us all hope again. Also, it coincided with the time when the sun began its return—most important for people living in the North—and the days grew longer, promising spring and warmth. So *Jul* was a holy time both for all the earth on the outside and for each of us on the inside. It was ever thus, he told me solemnly, from the beginning. The spirit gets rekindled every year as light, and is reborn as love in our hearts.

Happily and readily I began the gift for my mother. It was to be a little wooden box with dividers in which she could surely keep hairpins and buttons or the like. I knew that she had no jewelry, and now I realize that she must have sold it long since to help us survive. Andreas cut out all the pieces by hand with a jigsaw, letting me saw the longer bits, and he showed me how to set the little dividers upright and glue them into place. I was amazed at how deft his big hands were and how clumsy my small ones were. This enterprise kept me busy for hours, freeing him no doubt to go about his own work. He would hum companionably as we worked. He called his hums "*Julesangene*" or Christmas carols.

❄   ❄   ❄   ❄

The days grew shorter and shorter, and the darkness seemed longer and deeper. A great blizzard came and went, and for the first time the two trains—one in either direction—that rumbled through each day and were our only link with the outside world, did not arrive. The blizzard itself was terrifying.

I stepped out the door only once out of curiosity, and
without my goggles. Though I was probably only a few
yards away from the house, it was pulled viciously from my
sight, and I found myself in a furious pearl-white swirling
void with the snow stinging my face with sharp needles of
ice. I lost all sense of direction, became dizzy with fright
and gasped for breath. Only my piercing screams saved me
when one of the Englishmen came searching for me and
carried me back for a severe scolding.

"Lara," he shouted at me, "how *dare* you do such a
foolish thing!" We both stood inside the door, covered

with white and beginning to drip. His face was bright red and the snow started to melt off his mustache in a comical way. I didn't know whether to laugh or to cry, I was that grateful to be safe.

The morning snow stopped, and a strange silence began. The whole world was white—hushed, glittering and glistering. I held my breath when I went out, and listened. Not a single sound. The loudest thing was the awesome silence of the sun reeling in the blue of the sky. I closed my eyes and wondered if God could stand that much quiet and thought maybe that was why He made up a world so He wouldn't be so lonely. I think at that moment I felt sorry for God. When Andreas spoke about God, he made me remember something I knew already deep inside me, even though my parents never spoke of Him. It was all a puzzlement, but somehow I knew that it mattered. Then I put my hands in my pockets and scrunched through the iced surface of the snow making tracks with my boots. It gave me intense pleasure to think that I was an explorer setting my feet where no one had walked before. It was even a moment of time that was perfectly new and I could choose to think a thought I never thought before. Solemnly I put one foot in front of the other absorbed with the immensity of being conscious until I was summarily called in for lunch and told to wash my perfectly clean hands. I have not forgotten any of this.

My bedroom windows were full of frostferns every morning. One night I awoke to see flickering lights behind them. I climbed out of bed to see what they were, and when I opened the windows and looked out to the star-powdered black of the sky, I beheld the most majestic sight of my life. Vast curtains of colored light were swaying and dancing, tinted veils of beauty, waving and weaving in the heavens without a sound. They were the Northern Lights or the Aurora Borealis, only, of course, I did not know this. I was petrified that they might fall down on top of us and destroy us. I wanted to run for my mother, but my parents' room was too far down those dark corridors. So, with beating heart I braved the beauty by myself, my breath steaming out the window until I was too cold and shivering to stand there marveling anymore. And they didn't fall down.

During these days, I continued to work on the little box for "Christmas," the feast day of the Christ Child, which Andreas explained to me was important to all mothers especially. And he would sometimes lean over my shoulder and press my head against his leather apron in a rough caress as a grandfather might have done. Young as I was, I knew that my friendship was as important to him as his was to me. What am I saying! It wasn't just friendship, it was love. Love that we both needed so badly, love that was such a bright warmth in a cold world.

Then one morning the little box was finished. I had only to paint a design on the lid. I had thought to put my mother's initials on it, but something warned me that this might be dangerous, so I painted a border of little pink flowers and green leaves. Then came a coat of varnish. Seriously I bent to my task, brushing the good smelling liquid on and watching it transform the wood from a pale gold to a rich red-brown. The box was the first thing I had ever made and it was beautiful.

Gradually, a strange and wistful look came over the face of Andreas. He sighed deeply, cleared his throat, and told me that he had to leave to go to his own village. He would have to depart on the train and he might not come back. I burst into tears, right then and there, and threw my arms around him.

"Oh, no, Andreas! Oh, no! You said it was Christmas coming. Please, please, don't go away! Don't leave me!" I sobbed and sobbed as only children can, and I could see the tears standing in his own blue eyes. We had no idea how much we had come to mean to each other.

"Look, Lara," he said, trying to distract me, "I have made a little present for you. It is something magical, I think. It will help you to remember me, perhaps, after I have gone. Please, enough, my "lilla Lara," stop your crying. Hush, hush. You must be brave." And he pushed back my hair again and stroked my head, shaking his own from side to side in disbelief. "Come now and receive the

 magic gift. Enough with those foolish tears, come and look what I have for you." He went to his lathe, stooped over and brought from behind it his gift. It looked like a large sealed glass jar of plain water, but the lid was perforated and hanging down from the center of it into the water was a string. I was thoroughly mystified.

"What is it?" I asked, wiping my nose on the sleeve of my jersey, but Andreas did not answer me directly.

"Put this in your room where the sun will shine upon it and watch the string. Maybe the magic will come by Christmas and maybe it won't. I cannot be sure. But it might."

He made me repeat the instructions, and then carried the jar across the ice rink lest I slip and drop it. We parted at the door to the alcove of the coats. What a strange sight we must have made, the two of us—the sturdy old grandfather of a man in his leather apron and the little girl in the boys' knickers, holding her precious gift, a heavy jar of water. He leaned over and kissed the top of my head, held me close in a brief, rough hug, and then opened the door for me. I pushed through the damp coats trying not to stumble over the boots, blinded as I was by fresh tears at losing my friend.

In the manner of children, I knew little by nature of patience. I carried the jar stealthily upstairs and placed it on the top of the chest of drawers in my room, where the light would fall upon it. Then I sat down on the chair and fastened my gaze on the string, but, of course, nothing happened. I tried again in the afternoon before tea time and the next several mornings and still nothing happened. Soon, I was down to just giving it a casual glance. Perhaps it was too painful a reminder of my loss, and I put it in a corner of the windowsill.

Andreas had left that same day and nothing drew me through the coats anymore. The last time was when I stole back to get the little wooden box now finished and dry. The sight of the workshop all swept and clear and unlit and grey filled me with grief.

Fortunately, life in the snow-besieged hotel had become a bit more interesting. The last train coming through from Bergen had brought some more guests and relatives of the proprietress, and also a large supply of evergreen branches and a sizable spruce tree. People began putting up decorations in the dining room—red ribbons and silvery bells. Even I was pressed to the task of binding the green branches into wreaths with the help of wire and then tying red berries onto them. It was all for *Jul*, for Christmas, and it smelt delicious. In the evening a hot *"gloegg"* of spiced red wine was provided and drunk by the grown-ups, which made everyone more animated and lively, especially the dear Englishmen whose faces became quite red when they laughed, and you could see their yellow teeth exactly like old horses. My mother's knitting seemed to be taking the final shape of a pullover just my size, though she tried to hide it in her lap whenever I came in sight. It was dark green with white stars knit into it. I suspected it was for me but pretended not to notice. I was glad I had the little box ready for her whenever the time for giving was at hand. I asked her once at supper if she could teach me how to knit, thinking to make something for my father as well, but she said I was still too young and clumsy with my fingers to learn, and besides, she had no extra needles.

I continued to be mystified by the busy rituals of Christmas. I am sure everybody assumed I knew all about them. It would have been inconceivable to them that I didn't. My parents said nothing at all about it. My father continued to look wary, and though he drank some of the wine, he never drank more than half a mug, and his conversation was always commonplace. He never spoke unless spoken to; he never commented upon the political developments which, next to the weather, were the Englishmen's favorite topic of conversation. There was talk of war, their own experience of the last one, and of the dreadful need for peace. Much was said about reds and pinks and right and left. None of this made any sense to me. How could you fight a war over colors? My father received no mail that I knew of, with the exception of a large package, which I suppose people thought to be a Christmas box. It had arrived with Christmas seals on it. But I knew that it wasn't a present. It was a radio set that my father kept in a knapsack inside a suitcase at the back of his wardrobe. Once I surprised him in the bedroom by accident and found him with headphones over his ears. His alarm and my astonishment were so great, I was afraid of some terrible catastrophe. He did not have to say anything further. I knew that the safety of our little family depended on my silence. People underestimate the instinct of survival in children and their adult capacity to deal with suffering when it is shared with them. I always felt that they considered me a risk, being a child, but I never betrayed them. For most of my childhood a pall of fear hung over our comings and goings.

To this day, I do not know precisely what my father's function was. Perhaps he was some kind of secret agent employed by some group or government. Eventually, he simply disappeared in Romania. I have not the slightest idea what happened to him or whether or not he might still be living. I do not even know which of our family names was our real one. It must have been very hard for him to be haunted and feel hunted all the time, and even worse for my mother.

Finally, the hustle and bustle in the hotel came to a climax. It was Christmas Eve. Only about a fortnight must have passed since Andreas had left, but to me it seemed ages, and to tell the truth I had given up watching the magic jar since no apparent change had come over it. I had no idea even what to expect.

❋   ❋   ❋   ❋

The snow continued falling fast all day, and the Englishmen were thanking their lucky stars that the last train had brought them whisky and tobacco. Both were very merry all day long, and everyone suddenly began to pay a great deal of attention to me since in my small person I must have represented their idealized world of children. I had become a symbolic child and somehow I understood this. One felt dignified by this, but one was not to take it too personally. I know now that I reminded some of them of the child they still had within them.

The small dining room door was closed tight all afternoon, and there were all kinds of mysterious goings-on behind it. I sat in the front hall with my nose pressed against the window looking out at the railroad tracks, wistfully hoping against hope that Andreas might return for Christmas, but again the trains were not running, so heavy was the snow.

At supper time, the dining room door was flung open with

32

great ceremony. My mother made me put on my one and only dress for the occasion—a flowered dress with pink smocking across the chest. I had completely forgotten about the dress since it was a summer dress. Now I felt cold and naked in it. It was too tight and too short. Nor did my shoes fit me anymore, to my mother's dismay, and so I had to wear my thick grey wool socks without shoes as I was marched into the dining room at the head of the procession. I felt mortified, but no one seemed to notice a thing. Each Englishman held one of my hands, and they beamed at the beautiful Christmas tree all covered with tinsel and decorations with real candles lit and burning on the branches!

Then they leaned over and beamed at me, watching eagerly, like children themselves, for every sign of delight on my face. I am sure I did not disappoint them—it was a marvelous sight.

All the tables had been moved and set into a square surrounding the tree. We filed in and made a circle around the tree, and a man in a black frock coat with many silver buttons on it played the accordion.

We held hands and circled the tree singing a Norwegian carol with a very catchy tune. Not knowing the words didn't matter a bit, and I stomped my feet and yelled Hi! and Hah Hah! Hah! along with everybody else. People were happy and their eyes shone in the candlelight. Then we stopped and a prayer was said. Everyone closed their eyes for that, but I peeked and noticed some little packages under the tree in fancy papers.

When we sat down at the table, I saw that there was a tangerine in front of each plate with a little red candle burning in it and set in the middle of each row of tables was a splendid pyramid of fruits, nuts, figs, and sweet-meats. Against the wall was a long table groaning with a splendid smorgasbord—a glorious *fiske* pudding, *lutefisk* and *gaffelbiter* (codfish and herring). There were salads and cheeses—*gjetost* (a brown, sweet goat cheese) and *tyt-tebaer* (loganberry sauce), and *nokkelost* (cheese with cara-way seeds). There were flatbrod, and rye bread, and rolls, and pickles and sauces, all leading up to a fine Christ-mas goose which had been brought in with another fan-fare from the accordion. At the other end of the table stood a *julekake* (the Christmas cake, filled with currants and candied fruit). This, in turn, was surrounded by plates and platters of kringle cookies and fruit compotes for dessert. Everything was garlanded with ribbons and

sprigs of greenery, and every dish served was praised. As the party progressed, people burst into song and held hands and swayed to and fro. The Englishmen sang a duet and several encores which celebrated holly, ivy, and figgy puddings. The Norwegians roared with joy and jollity and joined in the choruses. The party got noisier by the minute and filled the room with love and fun. I felt overwhelmed and had to excuse myself and run out into the hall to the back door. I opened it for a breath of cold air and saw the snow had stopped, and the stars were out again. The great silence was back. The noise in the dining room was deafening, but I understood it now. God couldn't possibly miss all that noisy revelry. I really hoped He was enjoying it.

When I returned, I found that I had been missed. The men leaned back in their chairs with their pipes and cigars, taking a breather before more serious drinking of toasts, and the proprietress, who wore a most beautiful costume with braid crisscrossing her ample bosom, led me kindly to the tree and to the packages under it. My mother's pullover was the first one I opened, and it was greatly admired by one and all as if they had never seen it before. And I pretended the same and put it on gratefully over the cotton dress. Everyone clapped with delight and cried *"Vakker! Vakker!"* which meant that it was lovely. My mother also looked pleased with me and happy that I

appreciated the work of her hands. There were tears in her eyes when I hugged her with thanks. I ached for my father who now sat in the back of the room watching everything but not taking part really in any of it.

There were other presents from grown-ups I hardly knew—sweets, a box of chocolates, a small fountain pen, and a little book of Norwegian fairy tales. It was in Norwegian, but it had plenty of pictures. The Englishmen had given me two packs of playing cards and were eager to teach me a game that we all could play. They really were dears, both of them, sitting there in shirts and ties, all dressed for the occasion and looking properly aristocratic.

They probably never realized the deeper gifts they gave me, but I have been thanking them in my heart

ever since. Not a Christmas passes but what I remember their kindness, their noticing, their gifts of time and attention to me as a child.

It certainly had been an exciting evening and I was reluctant to see it

end and have to go to bed. But the
time had come and, prompted by a
look from my mother, I went about
shaking hands and curtsying good
night. Most took the occasion to
kiss me or pat me with loving
looks which I supposed to be all
part of *Jul* customs. With my arms
full of presents, I left the dining
room and went to my room thinking only with a pang how Andreas
would have loved it.

❋   ❋   ❋   ❋

When I got to my room, I quickly put on my flannel
pyjamas and "washed" my face with the cold cream.
Then I looked fondly at Alfred and tied a red ribbon
around his neck for Christmas. I got into bed too tired
to notice the moon now shining brightly through the
frost on the windowpanes. I closed my eyes and tried to
imprint the memory of the day so firmly in my mind
that when I grew older—as old as thirty-two!—I would
be able to recreate the memory of that day. It was fun
to make a date with yourself in the future like that.
And I kept it. This is probably why I remember it all so
vividly.

So this was Christmas—songs, candles, merriment, and gifts. Suddenly I realized that I had not given my mother hers, but tomorrow was Christmas Day, so it would not be too late. This was my last thought before I went to sleep. I had forgotten even to look at the magic jar.

I have no idea how long I slept. Suddenly, though, I was awakened by a short insistent tapping at my window and the sound of someone calling my name, "Lilla Lara, Lilla Lara!"

With a great bound of joy, I jumped out of bed and rushed to open the window, and sure enough, large as life, standing on the piled up snow outside stood Andreas. He had skied cross-country all the way from the next village! Down below, I could see his skis and ski

poles stuck upright and casting a shadow on the snow. The woolen tasseled cap on his head glittered with frost and there was frost also on his eyebrows and all over his mittens. His steel-rimmed glasses steamed up the minute he climbed in the window. He was a bit out of breath, but he whispered a laugh and gave me the coldest warmest (or was it the warmest coldest) hug I have ever received.

"Andreas! Oh, Andreas!" I squealed with delight.

"Shhhh! Shhhh!" he whispered. "I had to come to wish you a happy Christmas and to see about the magic jar."

My hand flew to my mouth. I had forgotten to look. But Andreas' first concern was that I keep warm. He closed the window and saw to it that I wrapped myself up in the down comforter of my bed. He told me to sit there while he checked.

"Where is it? Show me." I pointed to the corner by the window. He reached for it then and held it up to the whited window, and there hanging on the string were any number of crystals sparkling in the moonlight. Time had brought  this to perfection all by itself. I had never seen anything like it. It really *was* magical!

Then Andreas sat down on the chair close to the bed and holding the jar told me to look deep into the largest of the crystals. Softly, he told me that the heart of a person is not unlike a jar, and that we can have a string, if we choose, called faith. Then in life you have to be patient, oh so patient! These crystals took only weeks, but the real ones called peace and wisdom could take years and years to form. In life, he said, wisdom grows out of suffering and experience—yes, even things like loss, loneliness, and separation. But if you trust and keep that string called faith, you will find lasting jewels that make you rich and joyful in your heart. "And do you know what?"

I shook my head. "You can share these jewels with any one that needs them and who can accept them. Like you can, I believe. Can you tell me, Lara, why it's a magic jar?"

I thought hard. "Is it because it's something I can never forget?" I ventured.

Andreas smiled I think because it was not the answer he had expected, but he seemed pleased. "Maybe God made our earth and our universe so beautiful so that we would not forget Him. But we do, we do forget. The funny thing is that when you learn something from experience all by yourself or hear it in a good story, it helps you remember. Just a lot of words *about* something carries no proof."

I nodded my head trying hard to understand. "Is there a story about Christmas?" I asked.

He gave a great sigh of wonder at my ignorance. "Oh, yes, lilla Lara, there is a beautiful story." Then he looked toward the window and whispered half to me and half to himself the real story of Christmas, of the night that was so important to mothers because this was the night a most beautiful young woman had given birth to the Christ Child. (Everywhere in the world, in all religions, the birth of a little baby is a holy thing, he added. And there are other ways of telling the same story, but in the end it is always the same story—the miracle of spirit coming into a body that can grow up to love.) This story is the story precious to Christians, but it is for everyone to enjoy.

As he spoke, I looked into the crystals, and I could see it all happening—the parents, the long journey, the stable, the angels coming and going with shining wings. And I could picture the shepherds and their sheep, the cows and the donkeys, and goats and chickens, most likely. And the baby Jesus (for that was his name) sleeping softly in his mother Mary's arms with Joseph beside her. I was especially pleased about Joseph, because that was my father's name. And Andreas told about the three kings and their gifts and the star they had followed.

Then he explained that just as the sun comes back every year with more light, the same thing can happen inside people's hearts no matter what their religion. He said he was sure of this, even though he was just a

Norwegian carpenter, but he had given it a great deal of thought. If your heart catches this light as the crystal, it shines out of your eyes like love. And that is the true magic of the story, and this is what those three Magi knew, who all came from different countries, like Lara and Andreas even, and this is the secret reason they were called kings. And then Andreas tweaked my nose gently and told me that it didn't matter if I was a girl or a boy, that I, too, could be a royal person on the inside if I carried this crown of love within me.

And then for the last time, he held me close, brushed the hair from my forehead, and placed a kiss there that was a blessing as well. As he wished me a joyous Christmas Day and many, many more, he thanked me for coming even briefly into his life as had his own dear daughter, and he told me he would always remember me and most especially at Christmas.

This time I did not cry when he left me, because of the wondrous gift he had given me and because in my heart I knew it was all true.

✳   ✳   ✳   ✳

When Christmas morning came and the sun was sparkling on the snow, the magic jar was the first thing my eyes fell upon. It was bursting with splintered colored lights. I jumped out of bed and opened the jar and

pulled the crystals out and licked them, and wonder of wonders, they were sweet! They were like Christmas candy.

I rushed to get the little wooden box for my mother out of the drawer where I had hidden it, and I felt such a pang that I had no gift for my father. And then I saw the crystals and knew just what to give him. So I wrapped them up all wet and sticky in some of the Christmas paper that had held a gift for me the previous night. Before running down the corridor, I did look out of the window to see if I had dreamt it all. But, no, there were the tracks in the snow and four holes made by the skis and the ski poles of dear Andreas.

This was my first Christmas, and I am sure it is easy to see why I have never forgotten it or ceased to wonder at the power of love to come among strangers and make them friends—to come into the cold and darkness bearing light, no matter one's tradition or whether one is a boy or girl or big or small. I know Andreas was right. Christmas is for everybody.